Troublesome Trucks

Based on *The Railway Series* by the Rev. W. Awdry

Illustrations by *Robin Davies and Nigel Chilvers*

EGMONT

EGMONT

We bring stories to life

First published in Great Britain 2010
This edition published in 2011
by Egmont UK Limited
The Yellow Building, 1 Nicholas Road, London W11 4AN

Thomas the Tank Engine & Friends™

CREATED BY BRITT ALLCROFT

Based on the Railway Series by the Reverend W Awdry
© 2011 Gullane (Thomas) LLC. A HIT Entertainment company.
Thomas the Tank Engine & Friends and Thomas & Friends are trademarks of Gullane (Thomas) Limited.
Thomas the Tank Engine & Friends and Design is Reg. U.S. Pat. & Tm. Off.

HiT entertainment

ISBN 978 1 4052 69773
46670/8
Printed in Italy

Stay safe online. Egmont is not responsible for content hosted by third parties.

FSC
MIX
Paper
FSC® C018306

Egmont is passionate about helping to preserve the world's remaining ancient forests.
We only use paper from legal and sustainable forest sources.

This book is made from paper certified by the Forest Stewardship Council® (FSC®),
an organisation dedicated to promoting responsible management of forest resources.
For more information on the FSC, please visit www.fsc.org. To learn more about
Egmont's sustainable paper policy, please visit www.egmont.co.uk/ethical

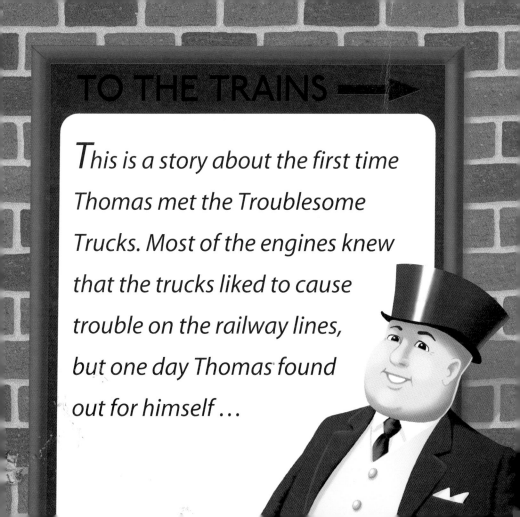

TO THE TRAINS ➡

This is a story about the first time Thomas met the Troublesome Trucks. Most of the engines knew that the trucks liked to cause trouble on the railway lines, but one day Thomas found out for himself …

Thomas the Tank Engine knows how to handle trucks, but the first time he had to pull them wasn't easy.

Soon after he had started working on The Fat Controller's Railway, Thomas became tired of pulling coaches. "I want to try something different!" he would puff noisily to the engines in the shed every night.

The other engines didn't take much notice. They knew Thomas was young and had a lot to learn.

One night, Edward was next to Thomas in the shed. Edward was a kind old engine, and felt sorry for Thomas.

"I've got some trucks to pull tomorrow," he told Thomas. "If you want, you can take them and I'll pull your coaches instead."

"Oh, thank you, Edward!" peeped Thomas, happily.

And all the engines got a good night's sleep, at last!

The next morning, the Drivers agreed to the switch. Thomas puffed off to find Edward's trucks.

He didn't know that trucks were silly, noisy things. They loved to play tricks on engines that didn't know how troublesome they were.

Edward knew all about the trucks. He warned Thomas to be careful, but Thomas was too excited to listen.

Thomas waited impatiently while he was coupled up to the trucks. When the Guard blew his whistle, Thomas quickly peeped in reply and began to puff away.

But the trucks didn't want to go. "Oh! Oh!" they screeched. "Wait!"

Thomas wouldn't wait. "Come on, come on," he replied, giving them a hard little bump.

"Ouch!" cried the trucks, as Thomas pulled them on to the main line.

Thomas was happy to be doing something different. "Come along, come along," he sang as he went.

"All right, all right," the trucks grumbled.

They clattered through stations and rumbled over bridges. The trucks didn't like being bumped, and looked for a chance to cause trouble for Thomas.

Thomas soon came to the top of Gordon's Hill.

"Steady now," warned his Driver as he shut off steam and put on the brakes.

"We're stopping," called Thomas.

"No! No!" said the trucks, naughtily. "Go on! Go on!" Then they all bumped forwards and pushed Thomas down the hill before his Driver could stop them!

Thomas raced down the steep hill much too quickly. The trucks rattled and laughed behind him.

"Stop pushing!" Thomas panted, but the trucks would not stop.

"Huff, huff, ho!
You're too slow.
We'll give you a push
to help you go!" they sang, rudely.

Thomas could see the station at the bottom of the hill, but he was going too fast to stop. "Cinders and ashes!" he cried.

He whooshed straight past the station platform. The people waiting there were quite surprised to see a little blue engine going so fast with a train of laughing trucks.

At the points ahead, Thomas could see that the line split into two tracks. He had an idea. Luckily, the way was clear as he turned off the main line and into a goods yard.

"Oh dear! Oh dear!" Thomas groaned, as he skidded along the rails. His brakes screeched and his axles tingled.

At the far side of the yard were the buffers at the end of the track. Thomas was going to crash!

"I must stop!" Thomas said, and his Driver applied the brakes even harder.

The buffers were getting closer and closer. Thomas closed his eyes tight shut.

But there was no crash.

Thomas opened one eye carefully. He had stopped just in front of the buffers! But next to the track was The Fat Controller, looking very cross.

"Why did you come in so fast, Thomas?"
The Fat Controller boomed.

"I didn't mean to," Thomas explained, meekly.
"The trucks pushed me down the hill."

"You've got a lot to learn about trucks, little
Thomas," The Fat Controller told him. "You must
find a way to make them behave. Then you'll be
a Really Useful Engine."

"Yes, Sir!" Thomas promised.

The next day, Edward showed Thomas how to pull the trucks properly and keep them in line when they played their naughty tricks. Thomas even stopped bumping them . . . except when they misbehaved.

And from then on, Thomas never complained about his coaches again. They were much easier to pull than those Troublesome Trucks!